ONE WILD PROPOSAL

Where's she going?

MARIE-ANGE SOMDAH

This novel is entirely a work of fiction. The names, characters and incidents portrayed in it are the product of the author's imagination. Any resemblance to actual persons, living or dead, business establishments, events or locales is entirely coincidental.

This book, or parts thereof, may not be reproduced in any form without permission.

YANIYO! BOOKS

Cover design by MA Somdah

ISBN: 2-915808-01-5
ISBN-13: 9782915808018

DEDICATION

To Mom & Dad, the Somdah's family
and my son, Sorwule Somdah.

CONTENTS

ACKNOWLEDGMENTS

Thanks are due to Barnabé Diarra, Mahamoudou Ouédraogo, Marc Pape, Koffi Yaboué, Achille Somé, Jean de Dieu Vokouma, Adama Koné, Kenedid A. Hassan, Longin Somé, Honoré A. Thiombiano, Laurent Magloire Somé, Jallow Mahtarr for being around for me.

PROLOGUE

At dawn.

Leaving the warm aqua.

Two sharp screams ripped the womb of the night.

Born into a troubled time. Crippled world.

The sunrise still holds a ray of hope.

The night was one extraordinary fight for a brave pregnant woman in labor, battling a thousand pains and a severe leg cramping. All alone. She could not keep pace with other women and children fleeing their town, running through the bush. She was left in a secret hideout used by hunters, all hoping to find her alive one day. Later, they said that a female captain of the national army found her. The pregnant lady had already managed to deliver two beautiful twins baby girls. But she died of exhaustion the following morning. The captain knew the father. It was an Oxford educated and an influential civil leader of the rebel army. The two twins were given to a religious center run by the Immaculate Congregation Sisters. At the end of the civil war, the female captain was able to track down the father through the services of the Red Cross and UNHCR.

Humanity still holds.

But human beings were always quick to destroy and cut those same hands that had set the pace to reconciliation and peace. At the start of the second civil war, one of the two grown-up twins was in the U.S., and the other one was brought with many others to refugee camps set up by the UNHCR in two neighboring countries.

1

THE LOST SOUL

Deep is the quest.

What was that furtive shadow in his dark eyes?

Why the forces of the universe have conspired against her?

Etana was already in shambles, entering that dark and claustrophobic tunnel, where a never-ending line of hope glimmered, fading here and now, and a mixture of knotted seeds running deep into her mind, smashing inside her stomach left gurgling. She had been walking days and nights following a tiny path through the green and dark scenery of the never-ending forest. It was dawn again. She had left the compound of her maternal uncle soon after the first cockcrow, leading her way through her past, stumbling here and here like in a harrowing dream. The morning mist was adding up to her troubled soul and vision, the dew refreshing her tired legs. At sunrise, the tiny point of the sun was still longing up there between the tops of giant trees. The overwhelming power of silence in the rainforest was frightening with all those invisible creatures staring at her. The silence was so mighty that sometimes she felt suffocated, but still her legs led her. As she reached a huge valley, tears were gone, leaving her face with the image of dried-up rivers.

Where's she going? ...

People wondered along her pathway, watching her graceful silhouette, and her beautiful and saddened face. Barefoot, wearing a fashion-torn jean and a T-shirt bearing the name and the image of a famous singer with his two fists up in the sky, she has become the wonder of up-country traders on their bikes or motorcycles going to the city. Even monkeys wondered about this beautiful stranger with such a grace in her footsteps. Once, a monkey landed in front of her, offering two bananas. Her smile was a wonder bliss echoing the beautiful trail of colorful birds on the move toward the horizon. The charming monkey jumped around her in joy, leapt into the air, then went back to a group of monkeys sitting on large branches, all gleefully clapping their hands. She smiled broadly and waved goodbye to the monkey's family. Then her face became dusky again, the skyline covered with many foggy questions. As she went inward, deep into the northern region, she had some strange encounters. She met the long gaze of a beautiful female farmer watching her flock. Near a water source, despite the wind and the muddy path, a long line of female traders was plodding on into the huge valley, she just left behind. Later, she found an enormous python sitting in the middle of the rugged road. As she approached, it slowly unsnarled and disappeared into the forest. Her totem was here to protect her from the web of evil forces.

The following day, she followed a road built for explorers digging for gold, they said. A little albino boy sitting by the roadside with an antiquated umbrella called her by a slow gesture of his hand, and gave her a loin cloth to cover herself, and a strong ointment to keep mosquitoes and other dangerous creatures away - visible and invisible ones. She sighed heavily, smiling. And the kid turned his face back to the silent forest, while the lonesome soul continued her harrowing journey.

Off the red earth road, she took a sinuous path, then crossed a village, people looking at her.

"Why she doesn't greet us?" said someone.

"No worry here! She is a lost soul from the city," answered another villager.

After three weeks through the rainforest, her body flagging, a cool breeze passed through her hair, and the sight of the big river suddenly appeared near a hillock. She had heard about the big river, when she was in primary school. Drawing near the river, she felt many invisible hands searching her whole body, and an intense internal seism mounting up, with lava spiraling towards her throat. She ran faster as she could, and started climbing the small hill. Up there at the top, overwhelmed by spasms, convulsions and fire, her mouth could not keep it anymore. She lashed out a deep and thrilling scream, her heart pounding uncontrollably. The echo of her devastating scream filled up the air and went all the way down to the lobes of her imperturbable grandma.

She woke up in the middle of the night, a beautiful moonlight above her, and a sweet melody coming from the distance. She stared straight into the night, trying to remember, to understand why she was in the rainforest. The reflection of the full moon had cast a mystical glow on the dark waters. It was a quiet and suave desire, but a malign one. She lay on the loincloth and went back deep into the night, lullabied by the rich and mesmerizing chorus of nocturnal insects; each group of insects with its own vocalization, humming, chiming, zizzing, ticking, under a full moon that illuminated the dense forest, silhouetting the big trees around.

The forest.

And.

The sound of silence.

#####

A nother day was crawling above the horizon. Standing on the hillock, she looked down the huge and infinite forest, and the snaking river still cozy in the cocoon-mist; and she stayed there, lost, unfulfilled, dirty, hungry, but determined. She contemplated the rising sun coming out. Soon after, the sky darkened, lightning flared and then the earth shook suddenly. Round after round of lightning and the mighty crack of thunders. The rain started pouring down, wreaking havoc, like there was a big hole in the sky. Her song was lost in the fury of the sky.

When the sun shone again, it was like a new day with a bright promise. But still she dreaded the day that lay ahead. She descended the small hillock, and walked toward the bank of the river. There she peered into the waters for a moment. Looking at the two pirogues, she chose the one on her right, and went down the river, paddling like all women born in the region. The pirogue gliding, she was thrilled by the amazing and captivating landscape on both sides of the river. Holder of a master in Film Studies, this could be the right setting for her second film. Her documentary *Les Jeunes femmes BIZI d'Abidjan* was a successful debut. The slight noise of her paddling in the waters was like dipping into the huge and mighty silence of the forest that conveyed a sheer sensation of ecstasy before the wonders of Mother Nature, and at the same time, a deep fear of the power bestowed to the invisibles.

Reaching her destination, she docked on the right bank, and moved the pirogue clear out of the water on solid ground. There were four pirogues on the bank. Her mother's village was thirty miles away by land. She felt a sense of relief as she walked, singing a local song that mirrored her daunting journey.

I am an ashamed soul

Covered by an ashamed body

Where could I go with such a face

Plunged into the shit of life

All tied up with the laces of abhorrent desires

Incendiary milk all over me

Killing my dear soul

Don't cry lost soul

Your grandma is waiting for you

To heal your wounds

And purify your body and soul

Don't cry lost soul

The end is near you

2

VACATIONS IN MARRAKESH

Outside there.

Outside your world lies the unknown.

It could be beautiful, though!

Etana had six options as part of a reward package for her outstanding contribution to the performance of the company. Morocco. India. Egypt. Ethiopia. Malawi. Singapore. Finally, at the suggestion of one colleague, she decided to explore one country of North Africa.

But, in a hot summer, choices always have consequences. She landed in Casablanca, and went straight to Marrakesh, the Red City at the foot of the Atlas Mountains. Exotic and mysterious were the attributes that summarized the city of Marrakesh at the end of her reading. She has learned quite a lot. The Almoravids, the Almohads, the souks, Jemaa-El-Fna, Essaouira. On-board magazines were always a delight during flights to get a first glimpse of her destination. She was a culture lover. Gazing out of the window of the taxi, she was more and more intrigued by the thousands charms of this historic city. The lobby of her hotel was a clear and magnificent introduction to Moroccan culture. The corridors to rooms were also a testament to a rich tradition. Beautifully carved doors, lamps, and wooden ornaments. On the left inside, at the sight of the courtyard, she stopped. Absolutely beautiful! It was filled with palm and orange trees, lanterns, colorful tiles, mosaics and one large fountain with two white turtledoves. Someone had advised her to explore the city.

On foot.

She planned to do so.

The beauty is in the detail.

#####

It was 5:15 AM. Time of Fadjr. Standing at the balcony of her hotel room, she watched the city still shielded by the night, the voice of the caller touching every house. The early morning was immersed in an oasis of blissful atmosphere. The caller's voice was so beautiful and divine like a balm of peace stroking her soul. She felt an eternity of happiness. Back inside, she ordered breakfast for two, and then prepared to go down to the lobby. At 7:30 AM, Viviane was already there. Always on time. She never missed a class when they were in secondary school. Sat in a quiet corner, the two joyful women chatted and ate their breakfast, composed of coffee, Moroccan touches, local bread and pastries. Viviane was free for the day; she had planned to show her around.

They started with the souk market in the medina. The souk is divided into areas for different crafts: Souk Kchacha for dried fruits, Souk Smata for slippers, Souk Haddadine for lamps and lanterns, Souk Attarine for brass and copperware, Souk

Cherratine for leather goods, Souk Kimakhine for musical instruments and Souk Sebbaghine for the wool dyers' market. Another interesting place within the souks was a small square surrounded by carpet shops and traditional medicine and cosmetics sellers. Rhaba Kdima. In the middle of that square, she haggled with traders from the countryside offering woven baskets crafted before your eyes or other authentic products from their villages.

The beauty is in the detail.

Walking on the streets, she let herself immersed in a completely different culture, more eager to explore and discover the genuine richness of this historic place. Each day she visited a different part of the city. Once, near the Royal Palace, she took pictures of storks nesting on minarets or flying over rooftops. Stork is a main feature of Marrakech's environment, and considered a holy bird.

Jemaa-El-Fna at night.

Saturday evening. Viviane joined her for a mint tea at Jemaa-El-Fna square, a huge square for many purposes. During the day, it was busy with storytellers, henna artists, snake charmers, musicians, dancers, acrobats, and monkey's sellers etc., and at sunset, everything moved to the sidelines and the square turned in just a few minutes into the biggest open-air restaurant in the world. They grabbed a seat at Café Argana for a cup of mint tea with pastries, before settling down for dinner on the rooftop of the exotic restaurant *Ksar Es Saoussan.* Jemaa-El-Fna was a testimony of the richness of a vibrant cultural heritage. This World Heritage site was definitely the place to hang out at sunset, a place where ancient traditions were still alive for everyone.

The beauty is in the detail.

3

THE KIDNAPPING

Joy of giving.

A blessing for the traveler.

For the road is a tricky one.

Two days before her return to Ouagadougou, she went back to the medina to buy some gifts for relatives and friends. She started her shopping at *Souk Kchacha*. She bought some dried fruits, and found her way to the silk and women clothes area. There was one beautiful dress, but unfortunately a red one. Red was a warning for her. However, she could not resist. Finally, she bought it. The merchant told her she looked like a singer in a musical video his daughter was fond of. Then shifting through the crowd, she moved to the next merchant. At one point, she felt followed by someone. There was this tall and well-built guy in a dark suit and black sunglasses. He kept appearing, too often for it to be a coincidence. The way he glared at her, watching her every move, gave her chills. She meandered through the crowd, trying to escape the sordid intruder. With the noisy atmosphere surrounding her in the main alley, she felt safe, but she had to go back to her hotel, where her friend Viviane was waiting to take her to Essaouira. Reaching the center of the souk, she made a call. Then whirling around, she dashed through the crowd as fast as she could. Glancing back, she breathed a sigh of relief, the bad boy hadn't trailed her. But, turning on the left alleyway, she found the guy; on her right, another man in black suit and black sunglasses was standing firm on the ground. Her heart started pounding, chills overwhelming her. She was scared as hell. The weight on her chest grew heavier, her breathing shorter. She felt her feet floating on the air. She ran as fast as she could, straight into a dirt alley. Then she felt a sudden and short pain like the sting of a scorpion.

#####

She woke up in a dark room with a poorly lit candlelight. The rough mattress had a strong and repulsive smell. Suddenly someone opened the door and started shouting at her. Furious like a hurricane. It was a black man in a classy suit. His accent was central African.

"Why you did not answer my last emails? He said ripping her beautiful colorful summer dress. Why?

"Who are you?" she asked.

"I gave you many millions last time. But I am not done with you, young lady! Every time I need you, you gonna fuck for every penny you got from me for the rest of your life," he hurled at her.

"Who are you, monster?" she asked defiantly.

He slapped her face so violently, she felt on the ground, crying, terrified at the prospect of being raped, tortured and killed. But still she had the courage to stand up and looked straight at him.

"Beware! The deep waters in that sacred forest is no playground for you," she said motionless.

He was taken aback by what he just heard, her soft and mysterious voice like something coming from afar. And the deep brilliance of her eyes hypnotized him for a short moment. He shook his head, wiped his face, laughed and headed to the door.

As soon as he left two tall and robust guys entered, lifted her and brought her to a luxury room, where she was tied up. She was in limbo, and physically exhausted.

"Water, please, water, please!" she cried out.

They brought a bottle of mineral water and a glass of fresh cocktail.

"You should reply to his emails, beautiful princess," said one of the guys.

"What!" she shouted. "I don't know him!" she vehemently denied.

They laughed.

"True! I swear on the head of my mother!" she insisted, her shoulders shaking, crying.

"It looks like you too met a year ago in Tanzania," said the other guy.

"Hell no! Never travelled to that country. You can check my passport in the bag," she added.

After looking into her passport, the two captors became perplexed. It was the same family name, but the surname of their captive was different, based on the instructions given to their boss a month ago. And added to their confusion, she was not coming from the US, but from West Africa and she was not a singer. Definitely, something was wrong in the whole affair. Confused, the two men left the house.

Soon, the captive felt awkward. The juice cocktail. She was drunk. A half an hour later, the young oil tycoon entered and jumped on the bed. He grabbed her. His eyes devoured her for a moment, hungry to satisfy his aroused beast. This time, no romantic music, just what he was craving for. He has found her. This time, he intended of setting things right.

Fascinated by her *bayas*, the magnetic powerful African pearls around her hips, he lost his mind, his manhood so pumped up it was hurting. She could see that in his face. All of a sudden he opened her thighs with force, and then she was ransacked like a house by the insatiable fury of a blind and ferocious cyclone. But the young man was not done with her. He intended to come back, in the early morning, at the first call of prayers.

The monster retired to a room on the extreme side of the old hammam, turned into a spa-hotel, where he was bathed by two pulpous young women, smoking shisha, drinking a cocktail made of vodka and some reinvigorating herbs prescribed by his personal medicine man from his father's village.

On the other side, the captive was desperate, unable to figure out why she was nabbed. Never met this monster. What has happened to her? O God! Have mercy! Scenes of the civil war flooded her mind adding to her abysmal misfortune. Was this related to her twin sister living in that faraway land? Or was this a punishment set by the spirits of her ancestors for something she did? Locked and lost in a foreign land, contemplating her fate. Why didn't she choose India or Singapore for her vacations? Fortunately, one of her captors opened up to an old friend of him working at the Congolese embassy, for he was troubled by the situation.

It was an odd night for the young oil tycoon nicknamed *Le Pétrolier*. After the soothing bath, images of geckos tortured him, leaving him in a delirious state. The images of geckos were everywhere he set his sight. He vomited all night some strange things of many colors. Something was wrong. His personal bodyguard brought him his suitcase. He took a medication and then slept. At the first call of prayers, he stood up, set on lashing out again his fury on the curvy lady for the sake of his already powerful oil and money empire. He intended to use her to get more rains of shining dollars' bills pouring in.

Time of Fadjr.

The monster was again at the door of the captive. He entered the room with a candle that diffused a powerful scent. She was still under the influence of the substance put in the glass of cocktail. Leaving the candle on a lower table, he turned around, his face lit up with a smile at the sight of her naked body. He did a tiny cut on her left arm, and poured a few drops on that area. With the captive's mind in limbo, the young oil tycoon started the final ritual. He untied her from the bed and flipped her over, and then open her legs. The fury of the beast was set to enter again into her private garden. All of a sudden, images of geckos started crawling all over the walls of the room. And the *bayas* went fluorescent around the hips of the captive. He stood there, hypnotized, his penis hanging flabby, scared of something just coming out of her secret. He retreated in panic and jumped out of bed. At that moment, someone knocked at the door. When he reached the door, he heard several voices. He opened and poked his head out. Three police officers greeted him.

The young oil tycoon was not aware of recent events in his native Congo. There was a violent upheaval that has resulted in a regime change that night. Informed of the presence in Morocco of the notorious son of the minister of Energy and Oil, the deputy of the Congolese embassy, decided on his own to call the police to arrest the young oil tycoon without talking to the ambassador. The two men didn't see eye to eye. This was an opportunity to take over. Everyone knew about the misdeeds of this voracious young man, the spoiled kid of the powerful minister of Energy and Oil of Congo. He was arrested and sent back to Congo on a special flight. The deputy of the Congolese embassy got a congratulatory call from the new president.

Someone got the chance of a new career.

Politics.

And its dirty game!

#####

The free captive was sent to a local clinic for care. The following day, she decided to leave the care facilities despite the advice of the gynecologist. She no more wanted to go to Essaouira. So long, Jimi Hendrix! A taxi brought her back to her hotel. She immediately packed her belongings, and headed to the airport, set to return home in the forest to heal her wounds. She was one lucky soul, but marked like a cowboy's cow with the seal of shame on her body.

Another ugly ritual for big money was stopped

just in time.

4

GRANDMA IS WAITING...

Mankum!

Precious gem, the root of the compound.

Grandma!

The limit of the horizon belongs to her.

The wise and the seer.

Standing in front of her compound, looking down at the lake, the old woman took her pipe and closed her eyes. A little girl in colorful dress came running, and took her hand.

"*Mankum*, come! The rain is coming again! And your umbrella is too weak for this rain!"

She looked at the little girl, caressing her hair and cheeks.

"*Mankum! Mankum* ! Where's she going?" asked the little girl.

"Who, my sweet darling?"

"The woman wearing pants!"

The old woman sighed deeply and walked back to her compound with her little great granddaughter.

5

HEALING THE BODY AND SOUL

The navel is the epicenter.

Rebirth from the source.

Mother Earth.

After four weeks of tribulations in the mountains, she heard the call of grandma. It was time to get the cure to erase, for good, the sully wound left on her body by that golden boy from Congo, her own sins, find peace, and then look for her lost love, somewhere in this planet. Where was her love? She intended to find him. Was he able to flee from his captors? What about her sister's lost love? The civil war was raging at that time. Through a contact of her twin sister, she reached the coast where a boat sent by the UN took her to a safe haven. Since those tragic events that shattered many lives in her native country, she has experienced the wandering life of many refugees, moving from East Africa to West Africa, wrecked inside with a family torn apart, trying to figure out what tomorrow has in room for her to chew. And she finally settled in the city of Bobo Dioulasso in Burkina Faso.

She arrived in the middle of the night, and sat at the top of the mound, contemplating the sleeping village under a magnificent moonlight. She easily located the house. She could see her on her wooden armchair inside her compound, swirls of smoke flowing from her pipe. She stood up, happy at the sight of her grandmother, then slowly went down the mound to the main square of the village. It felt so strange, for no dogs barked, like they always knew her. She knocked on the compound door, and helped herself into it. She stood tall with her cane and her pipe on the other hand. Overwhelmed, she ran into the arms of her grandmother, who laughed of happiness.

"I have been waiting for you my sweetheart," she said.

"*Mankum*, do you know about…"

"Don't say anything, my sweetheart!"

She interrupted her, putting the fragile and soft fingers of her right hand on her lips.

"I knew before you," she added.

This was a reminder of her mystical powers as a priestess. The old woman held her granddaughter tight, gently caressing her cheeks and chin.

"Come eat and sleep! Tomorrow is your rebirth!"

#####

There was an unusual atmosphere in the village. The dawn was surreal, but beautiful. Everyone talked about the return of the matriarch's granddaughter. A ritual was underway at the bank of the lake, the female twin surrounded by women. No men allowed. The healing and purification ceremony was performed every time a woman was sullied through rape. At twilight, her grandmother walked her to a hut near the lake. Four elderly women covered her whole body with mud, ashes, and male cows dung. She was given some instructions, then taken to the lake. Once immersed completely under the waters, the earth was shaken for a brief moment. A wind suddenly swirled above and hung over that spot, hovering, triggering a strong gyrating current on the surface and under the waters, emitting a powerful wave undulating across the lake. The women waited, singing and clapping their hands. Birds swirling around singing too. The sacred wind ceased. The cleansing of her body and soul was done. Emerging slowly from under the waters as the sun rose, there was an immense hoot welcoming her. A band of monkeys were all festive on the other side of lake, jumping and jumping. The elderly women pat her dry from head to toe with a special loincloth, laid her down on a raffia mat, and started a cure of special ointments all over her body and all intimate areas. Then they dressed her up, and she drank a calabash of pure water fetched from a water source.

A new day.

And.

A new life.

The village was ready for a long day of celebration.

6

THE LITTLE ANGEL

Strange, it was.

The forces of universe always play some tricky games.

Many riddles.

Just a wind. Scattered omens. Rolling the dice.

The wheel of fortune.

One evening, Divina invited some friends over for an African dinner. Later that night, after walking her friends back to the subway on

Huntington Avenue, she entered a 24H convenience store to buy a box of sanitary pads. Heading home, she felt a presence, and then the voice of a kid. She turned around.

"I'm your little angel! I will protect you if you listen to me," said the little boy in a West African outfit.

"Really!"

"Yes, Ma'am!" the little boy confirmed.

"Why little boy?"

"Because someone wants a drop of your blood for a pact with the devil."

"Hey little darling, you are too young to be thinking about these things! What's your name?" she asked.

"Little Angel, Ma'am!" he replied.

"OK Little Angel! But don't think about blood and devil! OK?"

Someone was calling. It was a well-dressed lady who was all smile. She wore a distinctive Nigerian outfit with a beautiful scarf.

"My little darling, please let the lady go home. Good evening!" she greeted her.

"He is so adorable! Good evening!" she greeted back.

The little boy ran and climbed in the car. As the Honda wagon blended into the traffic, she smiled at the little angel waving goodbye until the car disappeared into the night. Entering her apartment, she felt strange. The image of that kid speaking of drop of blood and devil haunted her for a while. Was it a real encounter or a vision due to her hectic and tiresome schedule of the past weeks? That night she woke up many times, sweating, in a state of trance. Something was looming in the horizon.

A warning hand.

Hidden in the clouds.

Of her life.

7

GLOWING SKYLINE AND PARTIES

On a yacht.

Somewhere in the blue Caribbean Sea.

Jamaica. The Bahamas. Total freedom.

Total addiction.

The paradisiac madness with no strings attached.

Divina remembered each island, places where glasses are cocktails and waves of wild desires that run deep underneath, setting the beach, the skyline and the body in a lascivious and dizzy mood, everyone vying for more electrifying carnal fantasies till total fulfillment. This flashback brought her to a mansion in Malibu, partying with friends after her arrival from Honolulu, where she had a wild gig according to those who attended the concert. Surrounded by her crew, she enjoyed herself at the poolside, dipping her feet into the fluorescent waters, sipping a cocktail made of tequila, pina colada and rum with a twist of mango's aroma, waving to crazy people inside the pool holding their drink and singing as the band played. Working the little crowd of the party, Denis arrived and grabbed her by her left arm; he hauled her to her feet and whisked her away. Surprised, she was rushed inside the big house to a discreet corner, where he made her regret coming to the party. This was a man so jealous, he could not sleep at night; his neighbors could hear him in a crazy rant over the phone inside his backyard. This is a man from Antigua swept away by an African siren he met years ago in college, his mind lost, like a needle in a haystack, completely blown away by her curves, always sneaking into her phone, smelling her clothes and her panties to detect an intruder's perfume and presence. O Lord!

She walked to the large bay window, holding a big cup of green tea. Sipping, her gaze riveted to the Charles River, her mind wandering to distant shores. She opened the door to the patio, welcomed by a cool breeze. Two women chatted downstairs. She could see the Hancock Tower in the distance. Two roving boats glided past in synchronicity. Then a waving hand brought her back to the street. It was a little boy on his bike.

8

THE WILD INDECENT PROPOSAL

Opportunities.

Choices.

And the two faces of gold.

Let's throw the dice.

Fate.

She used to walk through the fields at twilight, sometimes sitting at the top of the mound, where she could contemplate her sleeping village. It was before the civil war. It was then that she discovered the power of her beautiful and soothing voice; a voice that could relieve people's deep sufferings. According to a fortune teller, she was destined to worldwide fame. Yes, deep inside, she dreamt of stardom.

At Berklee Music Center, she was the model student liked by all music instructors. Following her graduation, she spent quite some time doing menial jobs, and playing with local bands. After many frustrations working with a blues band in a dark pub somewhere in Cambridge, not far from the Charles River, she finally got that contract with a local musical recording company, WonderSTAR Records. And this was the turning point, not only for her but also for the small recording studio, opening the door for many attractive musical ventures. Her first opus was all fire all over the U.S. Radio stations and nightclubs witnessed a memorable frenzy that went into a climax during the summer. Soon, she found herself jetting between Boston, Los Angeles, Miami, Montreal, Rio, Dubai, Jo'Burg, Lagos, London, Bali, Paris, New York, N'bi, Toronto, Accra, Tokyo, Luanda, Melbourne, Babi, Kin and Ouaga. Fireworks for a new horizon! Geysers of pulsating tempos!

Divine is her inspiration!

#####

On one freezing cold day, during one of the harsher winters in Boston, she got the shock of her life. The mail carrier has dropped one envelope that bore a stamp from Congo. This was an invitation by a secret admirer. 3 MILLION DOLLARS! Three million for a romantic weekend in a marvelous beach lodge in Tanzania. O my God! She stared at the letter, her mouth in awe. This could not be true! A joke! She lit up her tablet, and started surfing. She must check this out! She typed the name and company provided in the letter on Google. Perusing the Congo pages, she finally found the name of her admirer, a young oil tycoon nicknamed *Le Pétrolier*, the son of the rich and powerful minister of Energy and Oil of the Republic of Congo.

O my God!

What should I do?

She whispered to herself.

This was an indecent invitation, but an unexpected jackpot that could free her forever, free her from greedy record producers, giving her a strong leverage for her future recordings.

Oh Lord, help me! She wandered in her spacious living room. What's the meaning of a "yes" answer and a "no" answer in a situation like this? Standing by the window of her flat, she looked out over the river at the huge Kenmore Square advertising spot opposite her, and deliberated. She pondered, seeking an answer to that unknown golden hand that was trying to lead her ship to unknown waters. Not knowing what you want always bring unbearable frustration. This proposal threw her in front of her bathroom mirror, where she dug for answers about herself, her wants, her imperfect self, and her flaws. She never felt so weak and vulnerable, the opposite of her whole appearance. She came to the conclusion that there was something wrong about the sketch of her life. God's camera did create her beautiful, with a divine body that hurts men's manhood so badly at all corners of the world, sending pulsating and magnetic waves of wild desires into streets. Just imagine the walk of a beautiful crafted curvy woman! That's a sweet and burning fire under your rough skin. But this was a perfect picture without the right outline to live with.

She whispered, powerless. At the end of this deep soul-searching, she was still left to her own devices, looking for the answer to the wild and indecent proposal. Very confused, she decided to call one of her best friends in Maryland. This was too much to handle alone. Leafing through the phone directory, she came across the name of her jealous fiancé. Not him! Then she stopped thumbing, stood up and disappeared through the door of the bathroom. Finally, she removed that idea altogether. No, no! She feared being exposed one day, fear that this indecent proposal could come out printed in the media worldwide, about one greedy misstep.

This was a secret, her secret!

No one should know about it.

Never!

#####

After thinking over for a week, she decided to reply, just to acknowledge she received the mail. The following day, she got an email from her secret admirer thanking her for acknowledging, and hoping she will accept the proposal. The son of the powerful minister playing his chivalry added that this was a way to express his admiration for her last hit sung in Lingala, the main language of Congo.

She left Boston one evening before the next storm. On the way to the airport, she called her sister in Burkina Faso, and then felt quiet in a cozy cocoon, watching people on the streets going for their Christmas shopping spree. She had bought five beautiful ties and a box of cigars for the gentleman. She had her head in the clouds all day long. She could not get rid of that insistent and annoying voice telling her, *"This is immoral, so immoral! Have you become a vulture?"*, while an electrifying music was inviting her to a cheerful dance. She felt irresistibly deported outside the temple of morality. Logan Airport was bustling with people hurrying in the middle of colorful shops announcing the seasons. The plane was crowded too. And when the steward approached the door, she felt a strange sensation. Was she doing the right thing? Her mother wouldn't be proud of her. She waved her hand toward the steward shutting down the door, but no sound could come out, and she couldn't move.

"No worry! Everything will be fine!" her neighbor said to her.

"Thank you, sir, for encouraging me."

And the tanned and grey hair passenger added.

"I used to fear the moment the steward closes the plane's door, and I will utter the Latin saying *Alea jacta est!*"

Both laughed, amused. But still, she felt carried away to an unknown territory. On her own making.

#####

She arrived in Dar es Salam, the capital city of Tanzania, after a long fly with three stops. She checked into her hotel. On a business trip, the Congolese crooner was due to arrive the following week. She planned to visit the city to familiarize herself with the mood of the new environment. Everything was organized by the gentleman. In the following morning, she went out for a walk, then ended up in the business district, where she encountered a madman, who yelled at her.

"Hey young lady! If you are here for a good

reason, I shall welcome you. But if you are here to deal with a devil mind, I'm urging you to pack and get into the next flight out to Jo'burg. Do not sin for the bad reason!"

Really! So strange! And why to Jo'Burg? She laughed and called a cab passing by. Back to her hotel room, she found a note, a bunch of roses and a bottle of champagne, courtesy of the gentleman, *Le Pétrolier*. What a better way to set the mood of her first day in Tanzania!

9

THE DEVIL IN STANDBY

The prey just sipping the addictive syrup.

In the garden.

The devil and the prey together for the ride.

The sultry voice resonated throughout the night. *"When the devil had finished tempting her, he left her for a while until the next opportunity came."* Lush and luscious bodies chatting at the entrance of a famous bar scene for socialites. The city is a horny one in the night, a gentle and malign breeze stroking and awakening their animalistic senses from the waterfront.

The devil is in standby.

10

MORNING JOG

A few minutes before 6 am.

Time to shape the body.

Revitalize the mind.

And ease the day.

There are many running routes in the city of Boston, a true runner's paradise. But she preferred the BU campus running routes, including along the Esplanade and the Charles River. Her playlist was always a wonderful cocktail for her jogging. Richard

Bona, Chaka Demus, David Knopfler, Johnny Lee Hooker, Jah Shaka, FUSE, Nathanael Bassey, Labrinth, Victor Démé, P Square, Eneida Marta, Aster Aweke, Yolanda Kakana, Alpha Blondy, Teddy Afro, Papa Wemba, Tiken Jah Fakoly, Letta Mbulu, Ledasu Sisters, Ray Phiri & Stimela, Fela Kuti and his two sons Femi and Seun Kuti were always on the playlist to set her morning mood. She stretched both her legs out outside her building on Fenway Street, took a deep breath, and ran past two blocks of houses before reaching Boylston Street, and then took left on Massachusetts Avenue. The street was empty, but she could hear a whirring sound, probably from the highway. At the Charles River's bridge, she turned right and went down the pedestrian bridge to the jogging lane. Birds were chirping all around her. She was greeted by morning joggers along the river. She always enjoyed the early morning sports practice in this city, setting her mood right to take on the hectic days of North America.

She ran at a regular pace and soon reached the other side of the river, heading toward a block of MIT, where she crossed the bridge and back for a second leg before heading home. But she did not have the energy to go further. After coming off the pedestrian bridge, she slowed down and stopped. The wind whipped her hair. She breathed a huge sigh of relief like finally finding her freedom.

"Watch out!"

She found herself on the ground. The cyclist helped her stand up and inquired about her wellbeing. Luckily, she was not hurt because of the heavy grass on the side of the running lane.

Back to her duplex, standing by the window, for the first time she recalled one of the young women working at the Honey Paradise Beach Lodge's reception desk. Her name was Hazina. She was one of her fans. She knew all her songs by heart. She was sad the day of her departure. Divina vividly remembered that single teardrop running down her cheek that day. And by the way, when did her one-night-stand billionaire gentleman depart from the lodge? She said in a soliloquy.

She was at Julius Nyerere International Airport in Dar es Salaam. She remembered opening her velvet handbag to fetch something. She took out a piece of paper. *"Madam, I'm gonna miss u. Take good care of u, and please avoid this petrodollar guy. No good for u. Please call me if u want to know why."* Strange, very strange! Checking the hour's difference, she decided to wait until the morning. This was so strange! That teardrop running down her cheek was intriguing. There was something bizarre. Definitely, she must call her and find out.

What was beneath that wild proposal?

11

THE CALL

A bead of fear.

What was looming?

Was she ready for the boiling cyclone?

On the horizon.

It took her many tries to find Hazina, the young receptionist, on the phone. She was so happy to hear back from the singer. After inquiring about her twin sister, she told her the story of one beautiful young woman from Mombasa, who died in a horrific way after meeting a rich businessman who used feces on virgins and their intimate secretions to grow his business. He was killed by one of his victims in a bloody revenge.

Then.

Hazina dropped the bomb.

It was the shock of her life!

Hazina was working that night. They found feces on her body, and under her hotel bed seven strange eggs. As soon as the gentleman left at the crack of dawn, the security guard noticed something unusual. A strong smell coming from her room. Alerted, they went to check. They found her, unconscious with feces all over her naked body, and called for help. A traditional priest was summoned to the lodge. If she was able to wake up alert and in good shape that morning, it was because of a special oil diffused in the room after the priest has performed a ritual to get the bad spirit out of the area. And then, suddenly, the feces and eggs disappeared altogether. Before saying goodbye, Hazina warned her in a strong and unequivocal tone, not to answer any call from that evil person.

Also, she advised her to seek help, for she was sure that the guy used her in a ritual to get plenty of money.

When Hazina hung up, she fell on the ground, crying an ocean. She was thunderstruck by the revelation. Her hands shook. She couldn't utter a word. Her mouth had silted up. As the fear grew, her teeth began chattering uncontrollably. Dreadful tremors ran through her whole being.

She collapsed.

12

WILD DESIRES ON THE BEACH

The sunrise is a beautiful heavenly promise.

A prick and a golden bill.

Along the jewel of Tanzania. Zanzibar.

But the high tide could come.

Anytime.

A sudden whirlwind hit her that morning, when she opened the window. The scene of a couple kissing in the pool drove her to an African village, where she first met her lost love. The ring of her cell phone cut through her erratic thoughts, surprising her. The taxi! A bearded and fat man took her to the ferry terminal, about 12km from the Julius Nyerere International Airport, a 30-minute drive from her hotel. The vessel crowded with tourists departed for the archipelago of Zanzibar. She sat and relaxed on the upper deck, set with a private balcony, that offered a beautiful sight of the ocean. The journey took two and a half hours before the ferryboat pulled into the dock in Malindi, the ferry terminal in Zanzibar, at the heart of Stone Town. Right, after disembarking, she found the taxi area, haggled for a decent fare, before a colorful young cab driver took her to the hotel. Gazing out of the taxi window she felt like she had just arrived on a tropical island. The sight of palm trees swaying in the warm breeze, under a blue sky, was reminiscent of landscapes of Mauritius and Seychelles islands. And looking at coconuts, mangoes and bananas, ripening under the shadow of the large palm leaves, brought pure joy. She felt relaxed and happy.

Twenty minutes later the taxi pulled up to the Honey Paradise Beach Lodge. She was greeted by the manager and the whole staff, welcomed like a star. She was. Her international hit song *"Give Me Some Honey"* played in the lounge. She was delighted by the welcoming surprise and thanked the lodge's entire staff. As she walked to her room, she couldn't resist the charms of the lodge's environment. When she entered the room, she was in awe, admiring every part of the interior, her mouth wide open. The room attendant was amused. This was a well-designed African interior with genuine features from Tanzania. She dropped her handbag on the large bed and continued contemplating the decor. She touched all crafted artistic objects on the table. And all of a sudden, she ran out onto the powdery white sands. The view was breathtaking, overwhelming her. She walked alone with gusts of pure and fresh air pouring into her every pore. Heavenly sensations!

Back to her room, she wrapped herself in a large white bath towel and headed to the bathroom. A knock at the door. Surprised, she stopped and went to the door. A voluptuous woman stood there smiling. She was instructed to give her a special and warm bath, then a massage in the private spa room. Wow! This was her first time being bathed by someone since childhood.

The special and wild weekend started well with the session of spa. She was treated like Cleopatra. The masseuse was a sweet, sensuous middle-aged woman with a twist of Thai scent flavors. The bath was a beautiful moment, a sheer experience. She was immersed in warm waters, her head resting on Hannah's laps. Her hands were so sensuous. She first massaged her scalp and shoulders, then she worked the shampoo over her hair. A soft and relaxing music was playing in the background. She washed her body slowly with two scented bars of soap. After patting her with a soft scented towel, Hannah invited her to lie on a mat. There she started a full body massage from head to toe. The sweet hands of Hannah performed through every inch of her skin. The attention felt so good! She was pampered like a baby. She snapped. The voice of Hannah woke her up with that lustful smile. She thanked her for such a wonderful moment.

She spent the rest of the day in a blissful mood.

The gentleman arrived late in the evening. And at the crack of dawn, she was dragged to the beach for a spectacular sunrise, a sight not to be missed. The incredible low tide in the early morning at Kiwengwa Beach was well known and documented. They watched as the sun broke its way through the morning clouds, before sparkling on to the mirrored waters. Both were in total awe. She was swept away. A breathtaking moment not to be missed, not to be forgotten.

Eating her morning breakfast, the thought of making love outdoors aroused her. Fire prickled her skin. She always dreamt of the scenery. Beautiful beach. Sound of waves crashing. Blue sky above. Warm ocean waters lapping her feet, igniting her animalistic side. Gusts of air caressing her bared mons and intimate areas. Yes, she was craving for it! She walked down to their private beach in a Brazilian thong. Coming from the other side of the bungalow, the gentleman could not take his eyes away from the beauty walking slowly to their private beach. O Lord! This subtle and killing movement of her hips adorned with these dazzling and magnetic *bayas* and her irresistible curvy thighs.

He joined her on the beach.

Her skin was so soft.

Scooping a handful of sand, he poured it over her smooth and pulpous chest. He rubbed the grains across her skin and over her areolas. Slowly sinking to his knees, he started kissing her, traveling all over; then, he stopped and subtly took her bra off. She closed her eyes, feeling his hunger from the work of his tongue on her. Scooping again a handful of sand, he poured it over her bare chest, then he rubbed the grains across to her flat belly, making her warmer down there. He pursued his exploration of her voluptuous body, rubbing sand around her areolas and inward to her hardened nipples. The friction over the sensitive skin sent chilling sensations that went all the way down to her pubis, leaving her wet under the thin thong. When she reached to his manhood, it was like a hot iron ready to burn her deep. She grabbed it and licked his groin, toying around and enjoying every minute of it, then swallowed it, leaving him in awe.

The cool breeze of the ocean added to the scent of flowers, the smell of his body flooded her with a lusty desire that sent shivers to her clit. He went down her, between her thighs, eating between her moist folds, playing, stimulated by her moans. When the dampness gathered in between, the desire heated up. She pressed her pelvis against his mouth until heaven came down, her screams melting with the sounds of waves washing their bodies. She could see a powerful light she never saw anywhere in his eyes. Yes, she knew he was going to pump her the hardest way. She craved for a real one! But why this man? Or is it just for the money? She was on fire and wanted to relish the moment. She spread her legs wide open for him. Looking at the entrance between her irresistible thighs, his manhood went ballistic. Kneeling and grasping her hips with his strong hands, he then drove into her with such a hunger, triggering a scream that filled up the air and the ocean. Ecstasy was a definite reality to cheer for.

In the evening, a romantic candlelight dinner was offered to the singer and her partner by the hotel's manager on their private beach. The sunset was spectacular and the music a memorable symphony for the hearts. The perfect setting for a honeymoon. And the charm of his deep voice worked her whole body like soft waves of balm. A thrill surged and rendered her speechless. The first time she heard him on the phone, it was the same magical effect. They ate, chatting and laughing. Then they took a walk into the deep and soothing magic atmosphere of the night, arm in arm, entwined, contemplating the sea and its surroundings, and Divina dreaming about her beautiful sunrise on its way. Kissing was that door opened to the secrets of the night to come, where a whirlwind of golden petals and coins ensnared her body and soul, slowly and smoothly like a python.

In the morning, she woke up alone in bed. The gentleman was gone. On the table, breakfast was waiting. Lounging in the bathroom tub, the scenery of the night was surreal. What a ride! She smiled, then laughed. While patting her body with the soft pink towel, she noticed a tiny cut on her left arm, but did not pay attention to it.

She spent the day on the beach swimming, chatting with locals, and listening to new hits from various East African singers.

13

A SHADOW IN HER FOOTSTEPS

Beneath.

What was that shadow lingering in his dark eyes?

The boat to the archipelago of Zanzibar.

A sense of ultimate pleasures. Gliding toward a golden skyline.

It was a very special Christmas in East Africa. A memorable experience. Memorable for what? The outdoor sex on the beach or the bundle of million dollars dropped into her bank account?

She smiled.

The New Year's Eve was around the corner. She prepared to go to Montreal to enjoy the end of the year with her lovely sister coming from Ouagadougou. A group of old friends will join them for the fireworks. Outside, the city of Boston was bustling with people on the sidewalks and in shops. After parking her car on Massachusetts Ave., near the Christian Science Monitor, she strolled gracefully through the large esplanade of the Church of the Latest Days, toward the Prudential Center. She could see the big Christmas tree scintillating near the statue of the Chinese restaurant.

Entering through the revolving door near The Cheesecake Factory, she stepped on the moving escalator, emerging in the main hall filled with parents and kids enjoying the festive atmosphere of the season, looking for one last gift to take home.

She first stopped at Barnes & Noble Bookstore, perusing the shelves for the new book of the famed Brazilian author, Paulo Coelho. Then she melted again with the crowd, turned right at the corner of a clothes store, and went straight looking for Victoria's Secret and Lord & Taylor. These were her favorite ones. Yes, secrets and glamour! On her way out of the Prudential mall, she could not resist stopping by the California Pizza Kitchen for a quick lunch. She had a craving for pizza with avocado.

On the plane. First class.

As soon as she sat down, she locked the belt and opened the book of a new young author, *O Lord! I don't want my life shaped like a teardrop*; a title that threw her into a reflective mood. The voice of the captain announced the takeoff, cutting off her thoughts. She missed her sister so much. She wanted to treat her to a memorable New Year's Eve celebration in North America.

The plane took off.

She dropped the book, and her mind started roaming the streets of Boston, wandering through many places. Life is a book of many lessons one should read carefully. She had had many encounters, various faces from many walks of life. She recalled this beggar, outside a Dunkin' Donuts on Boylston Street, a former chief executive whose life suddenly broke into many pieces, he couldn't repair anything. Love is a cruel beauty. And that chess game between two funny dudes near Au Bon Pain around Harvard Square. "If you beat me, we switch wives" said one of the players. How stupid was the idea! Boys will be always boys! Having fun with anything coming across their minds. Many encounters during weekends where she was at the center of conversations. Her nightlife was a piano of many notes, black and white, spiced up with African flavors, like the menu at Mina's Delights in Baltimore. Sometimes, a flashback into Diomande Club in Paris would bring sheer memories too. But she has become a recluse, after breaking up for good, closing the chaotic chapter of her experience with Denis.

Since returning from Africa, her face has lost the sunshine of the genuine and confident diva. She retreated from the public stage. A tear would travel down her cheek, and she would wipe it, not allowing it to reach the ground. There was a sense of concern and regret. Her trip to Zanzibar had cast a shadow over her musical career. A malign cloud followed her, wherever she went. She has lost a lot of weight.

There was a furtive footstep, a hovering shadow on her every dream poised to strike her.

Why she did it?

She could not answer as the plane prepared to land at Pierre Elliot Trudeau International Airport in Montreal.

She felt that she lost her humanity.

Like her virginity.

In the hotel room, she recalled the maxims of an old book that echoed every event of her life.

"You cannot avoid the past you have invented."

"When the offer is too attractive and the answer too easy, leave things in the trash bin."

"Choices are your own making, so is destiny."

"Why one cannot dream of healthy human sensuality that warms the blood and freshens the whole being?"

14

A LINK TO THE PAST

Time never stops.

But time always reminds us of our misdeeds.

On the road.

Death awaits.

Something happened four years ago. The death of a singer in a hotel in Lomé. He remembered the city, awakening from a luscious and horny night, with its hordes of soaked and wild nightlife goers leaving the trendy nightclub Le Privilège, where all the jaw-dropper beauties ended up after eating at various restaurants nearby. This is a typical scene in Déckon and Agoè, two of the hot spots of the city of Lomé. It was around 6 AM, when he got her call. Thirty minutes later, the old cab driver was waiting to take her to an affluent suburb of the city along the coastline. The lady did not show up. He called her many times without luck. Suddenly, a car squealed and came to a stop. It was the man the lady met the other day. He was rushing into the hotel. The old man went perplexed. Later on, an ambulance arrived. The man reappeared totally shaken, in total disarray, tears flooding. Intrigued, the old taxi driver ran into the hotel to inquire at the front desk.

They found her in putrefaction, and larva coming out of her body. In the lobby the sad voice of the singer could be heard in the background. For the police, it was a plain mystery. On the streets of Lomé, they were talking about another victim of a ritual for power and money.

Love can be lost in a golden room

Life can be lost

Between my legs

Life is such a tricky game

To play with such a powerful

Magician, my Creator

God

15

SO CLOSE

Along the Gulf of Benin for a ray of hope.

For a cure.

But, time is a deceptive one.

Down an alleyway at a local bar called Le Sans Souci in Bobo Dioulasso, the Mandinka blues was a beautiful and somber bliss soaring from captivating landscape of dunes, intriguing knots covered by the charm of the guitarist that reminded her of Ali Farka Touré, a melody that left her heart lounging in a quest for answers. Etana was lost thinking about the putrefied body in the coffin with larva running all over. This was a terrifying way to die. What really happened to her twin sister? One acquaintance from Montreal said she was feeling really bad lately, and medical doctors in Boston were unable to find the causes of the scorching pain.

During a flight to Hamburg for her last gig, she met a film producer who advised her to seek help with a reputed herbal medicine doctor in Benin. As promised, he called one of his friends in Lomé to take her to Cotonou. At their arrival in Hamburg, the film producer gave her his card and scribbled the phone number of his friend on the back side. The concert in Hamburg went well, but she was so exhausted. Back to Boston, she locked herself in four giant walls, still seeking answers about her scorching pain. One Friday morning, she rushed into her room, looking for something. Back to the living room, she sat down on the sofa, holding a business card. When she looked at the back, she screamed out loud. "O Lord! O Lord! O Lord! Manu Tibenga!" She has just found her lost love after an eternity. She immediately called her twin sister in Burkina Faso, screaming of joy over the phone. This was good fortune! Both of them were thrilled. After all these years, they were so happy that he has survived the civil war.

This was the happiest day for both. Etana remembered how happy she was for her twin sister Divina.

But.

Hope is a mischievous one.

Etana left the café bar, crying and crying many rivers, accusing God for not being fair. She wished she could hear the thoughts of her agonizing sister, how she had felt about events of her life that have led to her sufferings. Outside, the night was sealed with an ethereal and eternal kiss from heaven. And that song from a local radio station started filling up the atmosphere with intriguing words.

When you become

your own ticking bomb,

scrolling up and down

along the spinal of life,

and time is running out,

the game is over.

16

ADA, THE BEAUTY GIRL OF ABUJA

Struck by tragedies.

Unbearable pain. Soul aching.

The wanderer. Head filled of knots.

Love still at the shore.

He was still inconsolable, sometimes sitting like a statue in the spacious living room, where his little brother and sister were doing their best to comfort him. It has been four years now. He had left

Lomé, after the horrible passing of his lost love that haunted him every day and every night, to reunite with his mother and siblings in Abuja. Saddened by her son's grief, the mother tried to find an answer to this ongoing ordeal, after the plight of two civil wars. According to a seer her son will meet very soon the other twin. Sometimes, hovering like a drone, his mind would start flying over the wonderful life and that absurdity of his affluent neighborhood of lavish villas and huge mansions, a wanderer looking for peace no place could offer, left to his own devices. There was no happiness whatsoever, living a king life in this neighborhood of Maitama District in Abuja. How one life is designed with tragic events?

Before the end of the year, Manu got struck again, this time by the gavel of the Pentecostal Church, leaving him again in an abysmal state. One of the leading figures of Pentecostal faith in Africa built a new and colossal temple to welcome his huge followers. Ada was sent there to do a counter-inspection of the new worshiping building. In her report, she advised not to use the place. There were some serious issues. Her report was mishandled by her own firm, and thrown into a drawer by incompetent and corrupted officials at the Federal Architecture and Building Authority. The direction of the church decided to plan for the inauguration day. But one of the local community leaders, fearing a collapse, implored Ada to attend the Sunday religious celebration, and check the soundness of the building, because he felt that parts of the edifice were unstable. She agreed. During the flight to Lagos, she pored over her own old report and looked at a confidential document emailed to her the previous day by a former colleague. She arrived at the event and was greeted by his host. As soon as they set foot in the building, the whole structure collapsed, burying many in the rubble, killing chore of people. Many lives were lost in the temple of God! Holy shit! One daily newspaper had this on its front page. HOW COME THE GREAT PASTOR WHO PREDICTED NUMEROUS EVENTS, COULD NOT FORESEE THE TRAGEDY THAT WILL STRUCK HIS OWN HOLY HOUSE? Another newspaper stirred the debate to a new direction, drawing attention to the fact that the architect who did the inspection was a woman, and people at the federal agency overlooked the conclusions of her report. The bright young architect Ada was rushed to the nearest hospital like many others. Unfortunately, she did not survive her head injuries. These victims were to be added to the long list of the daily victims, for the great heap of felonies and murders in Lagos was endemic, a sad reality facing other big African megalopolis.

Outside the sky was darkening as the sun fell behind the heavily impregnated clouds. In the distance someone was ambling toward the supermarket parking lot. Another crazy young man imitating the follies of young black Americans. He cursed disdainfully. A car door slammed. His young neighbors were back from their honeymoon, well dressed as usual, in a full Nigerian attire. That sight brought a beautiful smile to his face. Yes, the true Africa! And seeing the beautiful wife of his neighbor triggered a flood of fond memories. Ada.

Ada.

The witty and lovely sunshine.

And the gavel went down like a hammer.

Cutting it off.

It was in late August. He has just finished a round of meetings at the headquarters of ECOWAS. Grabbing his coat, he slipped out the door of his office, and headed for the elevator to the underground parking. Climbing into the car, he waved back to a female colleague, strolling nonchalantly toward her small Austin.

"Enjoy the remaining of the day Donna!"

"Sure, handsome man! By the way you still owe me a visit right? Here is my card!" she said.

She came forward, scribbled the directions on the back of the card, and handed it to him. He stuck the card in his shirt pocket.

"You never let it slip away, Donna," he teased her.

"See ya, you silly boy! Beware, I'm gonna cook you with all the essential herbs and spices available," she shot back.

Both laughed out loud. They always squabbled amicably. And he sped toward the exit door. Soon, he was on the fast lane of the new highway, on his way home to the Maitama District.

The day had passed in a blur.

At the honk, the heavy entrance door opened, and he drove through, parking beside a flower pot by the veranda. As soon as he parked, he climbed out of the car, greeted the gatekeeper and the gardener before hurried into the house. Taking off his tie, he slung his coat over the back of a chair, and trudged up the stairs whistling. He undressed and got himself set for jogging. But before heading down, he sat at his bedroom desk, rifled through the stacks of newspapers and stamped envelopes from the post office, then hunched over the desk checking his email box, pecking on the keyboard. A few minutes later, he stretched along his car, took a deep lungful of air and let loose, walked toward the big gate, and then into the street. Soon, he reached his running route and get it going. The air was cool. Back to the jogging lane after a hiatus of one week due to a conference in Cameroon, there were new faces on the trail. He caught the gaze of a young woman jogging on the opposite lane. On his last leg, the sky suddenly darkened with thunderheads filled up and locked, strokes of lightning flaring up above, and thunders booming behind with that resounding crack. Then the rain descended, landing heavily on the joggers. At a curb he saw the young woman. Another round of lighting strobes followed by a blast of thunder. She screamed and fell to the ground. He ran toward her.

"Are you OK?" he asked.

"Yes, but scared," she said laughing.

"Yes, thunders are frightening. Are you living far?"

"No! Just around the next curb, not far from the mall."

"I'm not far from here. Can you come with me to my house? I will drop you home? he proposed.

"Sure! Many thanks!"

The downpour continued as they ran side by side. By the time they reached his house, the heavy rainfall receded, but they were drenched, dripping wet. The maid brought a large towel, and she pat herself dry on the veranda before he drove her back to her parents' home.

One month later, he went to the new social spot of the city to ease his pains and relaxed. Sitting at one corner, he ordered a drink, thumbing through the daily newspaper at the bar. Then the bartender called out to him, inviting him to look at the far-end of the bar. He motioned, turned, looked up, and scanned the dimly lit interior of the restaurant bar. Someone was waving to him. After a few minutes, he stood up and sifted through the tables toward that waving hand. It was taken aback. He was the young woman that he met during one raining afternoon. Ada. She was a young and talented architect very appreciated in his professional circle for her guts, skills, wit, demeanor and rigorous handling of projects. From that evening, he found solace and unconditional love.

Ada became his backbone.

#####

The night had turned quiet, the winds stilled, the air hanging warm and humid. He poured two fingers of whisky and tossed it back, grapping the bottle again for another one. He had mourned the passing of Divina, then Ada. There was no fairness in God's plans. Scorching grief was eating up his body and soul day and night, every day that God created. He had lost several pounds. He was fighting for his life, assaulted daily by the unbearable pain, the whisky shots, and the midnight demons that carried him to Lagos bar scenes, where the nightlife was peopled by the breasts of high games prostitutes, rumbling the streets and electrifying the dancefloor. Lagos, that stone that had struck dead his new love! At that point in life, it was like he stepped off the edge of a precipice, and was in free fall. He has collapsed into an ocean of grief and alcohol.

17

THE CARD FROM THE TWIN

Music in the air.

The background of his life.

Soft with a twist of hope.

It was Thursday evening. The doorbell rang, interrupting his thoughts. Through the window, the gatekeeper was hurrying toward the imposing golden gate. It was the DHL courier. He signed the delivery pad, collected a small envelope, and brought it to his boss. Opening the rosy envelope, a soft and captivating perfume swirled, spiraling in the air. There was a card with a beautiful handwritten message like a poem.

My dearest,

Don't worry no more.

I will come to you next month.

I know your sufferings.

You already know my face.

I will come for you.

We will get married to honor my twin sis.

She will be proud of us.

God always has a plan for each of us.

Forever Love

He handed the message over to his mother sitting on the couch, and went to the other side of the living room; he grabbed a guitar, and facing the horizon colored by the lights of the city, he started playing. Her mother closed her eyes, her hands on the head of her daughter resting on her laps, tears running down their cheeks.

18

FROM BOBO DIOULASSO

When you are lost.

You dream of hope. Just a single ray.

When you lost everything. That stupid war!

You dream of an open door.

With welcoming hands and hearts of love.

A new home.

Sunday morning. Etana decided to skip Le Dankan, her habitual breakfast spot. She was calm but a little bit apprehensive of that upcoming meeting in

Ouagadougou. Meeting Manu, the lost love of her late twin sister. And it was always difficult for her each time she had to leave her beloved city of Bobo Dioulasso. After completed her film studies at the Film Institute of Ouagadougou, she settled in Bobo. Her discovery and love of Bobo Dioulasso dated back to her first trip as a student to observe three days of film shooting. Since then, this city has become a delight for her. It was there that she spent her time working on the script of her documentary. She loved the quiet atmosphere, the architecture of the train station, the old Mosk of Dioulassoba built during the 19th century, the new Maison de la Culture, Le Dankan restaurant, and the twist to La Guinguette in Nasso, a few miles from the city, was always welcome. She also enjoyed grabbing a seat at the terrace of a café bar or *maquis* to have a drink and a good laugh. Sometimes, she played chess games on sidewalks or enjoyed the ritual of sipped tea called *grin* in the neighborhood. The quiet and cool atmosphere of this city made it her much loved city in West Africa. And there was always that string of kora's notes and the melody of balafon brought to her ears by the cool breeze coming from Bolomakoté in the evening.

Drinking her cup of coffee with local pastries made of soy flour, savoring every mouthful on the rooftop terrace of Le Dafra, a new coffee shop versed in arts and crafts, she jotted down a few lines on her yellow notepad, then thinking about her trip to Ouagadougou the following day, she was struck by the pulse of a *djembé* and a familiar voice from the street that took her miles away to a village, where she used to go on weekends. She would jump on her motorbike and set forth to be with him. She remembered the last time she returned there. The house was still there, sat in the green valley along the quiet river. It was Friday evening. She drove slowly, the headlights shining out into the dark, in the middle of nowhere, her mind navigating between the tall grass on both sides of that potholed dirt road. The corroded gate still hung there. She pulled the car in beside the house, and stepped out. She looked around, breathed a cool air from the night, and slowly walked to the house. In the dark, she fumbled with the keys, then lit up her smartphone. She opened the door and went inside. The damp musty air hung still and heavy. She walked around the house, the flashlight of her phone opening up the box of the past. Dust lay thick on the floors, and cobwebs on all corners of the living room like decorative items. When she opened the door of the bedroom, a strong musty smell invaded her nostrils, quickly erased at the sight of her portrait beautifully painted by him, the genius of arts. Tears started flooding down her cheeks. Sitting on the mattress, her right hand went on to grab a document. It was a manuscript. She started reading in astonishment. Oh my God! It was a biography about her. She cried, her shoulders shaking uncontrollably.

Suddenly, a violent thunder cracked the sky and slammed a door, closing the memory lane, and the unbearable sequence of his accident immediately removed from her thoughts. Up there, thunderheads shattered the sky, and the color of menacing clouds sent people hurrying away to any shelter they could find. As soon as she left the terrace, the rain went havoc. She found a table at a quiet corner, where she sat down and ordered a drink. The smile of the waitress with her beautiful nappy hair was like a positive echo reverberating in her; she wore a T-shirt with the image of Thomas Sankara and a beautiful crafted necklace. She asked her where she could buy the T-shirt like the one she was wearing. And she was amused when the waitress asked about her own T-shirt with the image of Fela. Etana was a nappy gal too, a staunch advocate of natural hair, and a fiery opponent of skin bleaching. Once, an old woman she met at a local market told her she was beautiful like Mother Earth. After thumbing the daily newspaper, she stood up slowly and walked to the window, and contemplating the rain, she got carried away to many places, a *reverie* that was a testimony to her bachelor life; the unbearable true of a life spiced up with many men, unable to find again that special star that was brightening her life. Once, the wind of cupidon took her to La Guinguette, the Cascades de Karfiguéla near the city of Banfora, the marvelous Campement de Thialy in the peninsula of Thialy, before she was swept off her feet and brought south to the beautiful landscape of Cape Coast by a gentleman from Hamélé, the city-frontier of Burkina Faso and Ghana. It was a sudden sultry tornado under her skin, and she was lucky to get out of that season of unknown and uncontrollable desires that made her look insane at the end of that journey into wilderness pleasures. The nappy gal was still a bachelor, but a happier one, who has learned about her flaws and became a stronger being.

Outside, the rain was receding slowly.

#####

Monday morning. The strings of kora and the notes of balafon and prayers, all brought by a cool breeze. The road awaited her. She decided to leave the city by driving up the long Boulevard Eboué, enjoying the morning scenes of city dwellers on both sides of the street. At the roundabout called Place de la Femme, she turned left on Route 1, the road to Ouagadougou. The music of Hawa Boussim was playing in the background.

The playlist was always an important part of her driving, with local, West African and international flavors. Baba Commandant, Solo Dja Kaboco, Peter Gabriel, Pédro Kouyaté, Batal Pulaaku, Vieux Farka Touré, Asa, David Tayorault, Van Morrisson, Sona Jobarteh, Cabrel, Freeman Tapily, Sidiki Diabaté, Floby, Yemi Alade, Flavour, Oumou Sangaré, Elie Kamano, Nessa, Seun Kuti, Amadou Ballaké, Lokua Kanza, Dicko Fils, Josey, Abdoulaye Diabaté et les

Younkouna, Idak Bassavé, Frère Malkhom, Toofan, Sandra Mbuyi, Charlotte Dipanda. It took her five hours drive on the new beautifully crafted asphalt road. Years ago, it was a cumulus of red dust behind the car on a potholed road, where you always ended up with a flat tire. She remembered how difficult it was to drive then. She never rushed, taking the time to enjoy the road, the sight of beautiful landscapes, chatting with people along the way and learning about their traditions and stories. Houndé, Pa, Ouahabou, Boromo, Sabou. Mastering three local languages, she was at ease anywhere she set foot. After a short stop to see the sacred crocodiles of Sabou, she arrived in Ouaga around 5 PM and checked into a small hotel not far from the central market Rood Wooko. Dropping her handbag on the bed, she could not resist grabbing a beer in the small fridge to cool down. Later that evening she spent a lively time with friends at Taxi Brousse near Cappuccino and Splendid Hotel on Avenue Kwame N'Krumah, then at I-kodi Café, another outdoor restaurant typical of Ouaga, with the best delicious grilled chicken and juicy sheep skewers in town, spiced up with cool beer and good reggae vibrations.

When the taxi dropped her at the hotel, it was midnight.

The quiet atmosphere of the room brought her into a reverie along the footsteps of her life, the enduring footnotes engraved on stones all over the shoreline. The past was not an eloquent play to share. She had, now, experienced that horrific cataclysm inside her own body. Suddenly, everything had fallen apart, leaving her in the rubble and ruins. The ordeal of rape during her vacations brought back the savagery of the civil wars, and the trauma endured by many women. The magnitude of this seism could not be measured, for she was left dulled, locked in a state of appalling apathy, living a spectral life for two years. She was burned to her very soul. There was no road into the future, as she sighed deeply.

She had been so much hurt, that something inside her had vanished, perished in the ashes of human evilness. Some of her feelings had gone. She had spent many years insentient, removed from the social life. This had been a tragic and trying time for her.

And one night, she heard whispers from the

sweet and soothing voice of her *mankum*, her grandma. She was telling her to keep on moving, no matter how many skies have fallen on her. The following morning, as she remembered vividly, she felt a new energy flowing into her whole being. She was set for a new dawn, a new beginning that led up to a new love, a remarkable artist, whom wisdom empowered her, bringing her star back in full gear. Every encounter in life has a purpose.

Joining her palms together over her forehead, she prayed fervently, thanking God for her resilience. Then she slipped into her nightdress and went to bed with the morning meeting in mind.

19

A NEW BEGINNING

Sunrise.

The future still holds. And that could make for an odd feeling.

Building from the ghost's spirit of a lost love.

Looking at the relics.

And still believing in the possibility and the magic of love.

In a deserted location of a quiet neighborhood, something was lingering in the air. Two souls in a quest. The old cab driver felt it too. The past was calling. The car stopped in a vast and empty area like a soccer field. The old man got out of the car to open the door. Etana slid out of the taxi and thanked him. When she looked up, she noticed a car far away close to the horizon, and someone came out of it, and started moving slowly toward them. He has arrived during the night from Abuja. The cab driver watched her walking with such a grace, and wondered where he met this attractive lady for the first time. As Etana was approaching the man, she could hear music playing in the distance. Tears started flooding out, running down, numerous flashbacks shaking her. It was one of her sister's song, a song dear to her soul. Overwhelmed, she stumbled on an invisible wall of clouds, then stopped. Their eyes met. One could capture the essence of that moment, memories flushing out from different angles. An eternity!

"Why! Oh God, why!" she screamed.

Her hands up touching the sky, her shoulders were shaken by a powerful pain coursing along her spine.

The old cab driver was watching the scene, praying. He had witnessed many things, bad and good, while driving people around the city. But this one was an unusual one by the atmosphere, the time of the day. He met the lady at the airport. She was just out of the immigration and customs checking point with her luggage in a cart, looking for a cab. A quick flash from a civil war. She looked like his late wife, when she was younger, a beautiful woman with such an attractive aura. He greeted her and took her cart to his taxi. At the hotel, she paid and scribbled the cab driver's phone number down her yellow pad. She had planned to meet someone the following day.

Something from the past was definitely part of this morning drama. The old cab driver was himself immersed in a quest, finding the nieces of his late wife. A flash thundered like a spray of bullets, and an echo came from the past. A sharp pain sliced through him. The first civil war. What was the origin of this beautiful face? Years ago, right? It was four years ago, before he moved to Burkina Faso. Yes, he remembered now, but his thoughts were interrupted by a lighting, and his eyes went back to the odd couple. Suddenly, in an amazing synchronicity, the two souls walked toward each other at the middle of the field, and then melted. It was a deep and captivating moment rendered sublime by the tone of the sunrise and the song of birds.

Etana was happy for her twin sister. Divina could now rest in peace. Ada had predicted this reunion for Manu.

20

CRASHING HIS MANHOOD

Don't.

Do not let them go angry.

Otherwise, you should start hiding your tail.

Between your legs.

Beware of the fury of spatulas.

In court, *Le Pétrolier* told the judge he didn't know his female conquests were set to die after he had sex with them. Liar! Liar! Liar! The judge had to warn people against interrupting the proceedings.

According to one of his pals, his friend was trying to create his own oil empire. For that purpose, he secretly met a "marabout", who has helped many other entrepreneurs. Outside the central court, there was a huge crowd, mostly women with their spatulas. They were shouting, screaming all over the place, contained by the police. They wanted the judge to throw the young oil tycoon on the street, so that they could give him the right punishment for his crimes. His father was on the run. The splendid mansion of the minister of Energy and Oil was ransacked, and burned down to ashes. Three million dollars for a weekend of sex delight! This was an abhorrent crime they could not condone. Enough of these cynical and arrogant politicians, and their rotten offspring, playing with government money. The women were in a bowl of fury chanting. The dreadful waves of spatulas from the seven regions of the country and beyond the national borders were ashore, warming up, before the Citadel. The cyclone was set to unleash its inner power.

Where is our money, stolen from state funds?

Bring it back here

Where is our money eaten by their wives

and a thousand of cupid mistresses?

Bring it back here, where you stole it

Where is that money wasted all over the world

By their rotten offspring?

Bring it back here, where you stole it

Where is our money, you, the vile plunderers?

Bring it back here, where you stole it

Where is our money?

Bring it back now, there, to the place you stole it

Before the final judgement

Locked up at the Central Correctional Center, *Le Pétrolier* suffered from a mysterious illness transmitted by a rare type of gecko. Black spots appeared on his skin. When did that happen? He then recalled his nightmarish night in Marrakesh with the image of geckos wandering on the walls and in his dreams. Many questions ran through his mind. Why he missed that conference on geckos, when he was a student at the School of Sciences. Why? But what scared him to death, being hit in his genitals with a spatula. For good reason. It is said that if a woman hit your manhood with her spatula, it's a curse. When African women are on the streets with their spatulas, the president and his regime are in serious troubles. It means the end is near. So concern rippled through him. He was afraid of female inmates looking at him, winking, and smiling at that handsome and rich man. He finally decided not to go alone for his daily walks, for fear of being hit with a spatula.

What's next for him?

The judgment of the male order or the judgment of the spatulas? After four months in jail, *Le Pétrolier* became thin and walked like a duck in a large African outfit. The medical doctor of the prison was trying hard to cure his swollen testicles that hurt so badly. The old hamman of Marrakesh haunted him every night with bizarre and frightening sex parties with a beautiful woman, whose body was covered with grey spots like geckos. At the end of each sex session, he will wake up, naked, terrified, screaming. Each night will bring a new burning spot on his body, the mark of a slow and unbearable punishment. One of his former associates strongly supported the idea that the young oil tycoon was hit by a malediction, a powerful spell flowing from the *bayas* of that young woman kidnapped in Marrakesh. He even went further, saying that his pal slept with the negative double of that woman in Marrakesh.

EPILOGUE

A new morning shall rise.

The question is there.

Song of spatulas, fierce voices.

Let's hope!

No more of it!

According to the old wise man, the time of the power of spatulas has come. Something was hanging up there like a new song, a new dawn sprinkled with the charms of *bayas*, for rebirth means sacrifice of the Old Order. Yeah! I immediately took my hand off the attractive waitress's waist, where I could feel her *bayas* calling my basic instincts. I emptied my glass of whisky and headed to the door.

Outside the bar, Le Dernier Sou, I walked to my moto and cruised into the night, leaving many weekend goers trapped in their heavy thoughts, sipping their whisky or beer, contemplating the bottom of scattered bottles on the table, their hearts lullabied by the moving voice of Victor Démé, their bodies invaded by the voracious hands of night beauties with their *bayas* ready for their preys. This could be an interesting setting to start a new story.

October 12, 2019 – Pissy, Ouagadougou (Burkina Faso)

Marie-Ange Somdah

ALSO BY MARIE-ANGE SOMDAH

The Dream of Little Awa. Boston, Ouagadougou : Yaniyo! Books, 2013.

Le Rêve de la petite Awa. Paris : Edilivre, 2013.

Pen & Dreams from My Students. Boston, Ouagadougou : Yaniyo! Books, 2013.

Libertés, chocolat & cie. Paris : Le Manuscrit, 2005.

Images de vie. Paris : Le Manuscrit, 2005.

Un long fleuve. Paris : Le Manuscrit, 2005.

Hôtel la Désirade & autres récits. Le Manuscrit, 2005.

Un Soleil de Plomb. Paris : L'Harmattan, 2003

Rêves de Savane. Boston, Ouagadougou : Yaniyo! Books, 2002.

Seeds & Deep Seasons. New York : Mellen Press, 2009.

Campus Blues. Paris : Nouvelles du Sud, 1998.

Le Nombril de la terre. Paris : L'Harmattan, 1994.

Adjoa, l'Aurore. Besançon : Couleur Locale, 1992.

Demain sera beau. Paris : Silex, 1989.

ABOUT THE AUTHOR

Marie-Ange Somdah is a poet, bilingual writer, novelist, educator and professor from Burkina Faso, based in Boston. The author of *Seeds & Deep Seasons (1997)*, first printed by Mellen Press, he has published several books in English and French, including children's books *Rêves de Savane (2002)*, *The Dream of Little Awa (2013)* and *Le Rêve de la petite Awa (2013)*.

Trained in Burkina Faso (Université Joseph Ki-Zerbo), France (Université de Franche Comté) and the USA (Boston University School of Education and Harvard University Extension), he has taught at various universities in the US and Africa. As part of his commitment to volunteering, he has provided free writing workshops for students and communities in various settings. He has edited and published *Pen & Dreams from My Students (2013)*, a collection of works by his students. In addition, his writing workshops for women's empowerment organized for Women's Day in Djibouti (Horn of Africa) was supported with certificates and awards given by IFESH and USAID to recipients.

Also known for his international educational development work and achievements, he was twice honored with the *Teachers For Africa Award (TFA)* in 1998 and 2008 for his endeavors in Benin and Djibouti by IFESH, an American NGO.

Marie-Ange Somdah is currently designing new curricula for African private universities, and helping build new ones. A passionate of jogging, drawing, painting, music and photography, like his son, he is a soccer lover.

* 9 7 8 2 9 1 5 8 0 8 0 1 8 *